# *Almost Famous Daisy!*

## Richard Kidd

SIMON & SCHUSTER
BOOKS FOR YOUNG READERS

# Famous
## PAINTING COMPETITION

## Paint Your Favorite Things
## Win 1st Prize
## Be Famous!

## All paintings must be submitted
## no later than Monday, April 1st

## The judges' decision will be final

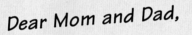

Dear Mom and Dad,

We're off to find my favorite things!
We're going to paint the world!
I know you will be very proud of me
if my picture wins a prize in the contest.
Don't worry, Duggie and I will send you
postcards from all the places we visit.

Love,        Daisy

Duggie

X

FRAN

Daisy and Duggie arrived in France on Monday, and by evening they were in Saint-Rémy. By the time Daisy finished unpacking, it was already dark, and an owl was hooting in an almond tree. She and Duggie climbed to the top of a tall hill, where they could almost touch the stars! Daisy felt so inspired, she set up her paints and easel and started to work.

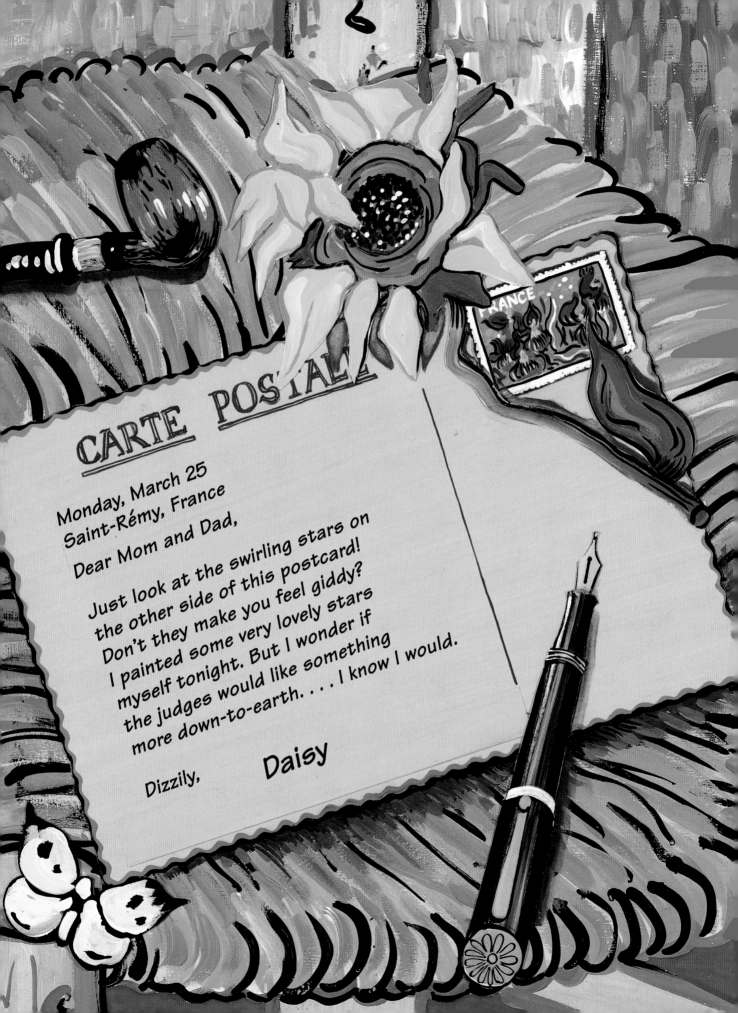

CARTE POSTALE

Monday, March 25
Saint-Rémy, France

Dear Mom and Dad,

Just look at the swirling stars on
the other side of this postcard!
Don't they make you feel giddy?
I painted some very lovely stars
myself tonight. But I wonder if
the judges would like something
more down-to-earth. . . . I know I would.

Dizzily,        Daisy

*The Starry Night* (1889) Vincent van Gogh

HÔTEL
Claude

27

On Tuesday, Daisy and Duggie traveled to Rouen
and found a hotel right in the middle of town.
The day was gray and it looked like it might rain,

so Daisy and Duggie stayed inside, where Daisy painted the view from her window—a huge church called Rouen Cathedral.

Tuesday, March 26
Rouen, France

Dear Mom and Dad,

Rouen Cathedral is really impressive, and so is Monet's painting of it (see the other side of this postcard)! I had a hard time painting my picture, because the light keeps changing here. I'm sticking to landscapes from now on!

Decidedly,      Daisy

MUSÉE DES BEAUX-ARTS, ROUEN.

ROUEN TOURS
ST-RÉMY A RO

FRANCE

Hotel Daisy

*Rouen Cathedral, the Portal and the Tour Saint-Romain:*
*Morning Effect, Harmony in White*
(1893) CLAUDE MONET

Daisy and Duggie caught a train to Belarus, and by late Wednesday, they were settled at an inn at Vitebsk. Daisy fell in love with Belarus—it was very poetic.

She could smell the pine forest and hear the geese honking. Duggie felt poetic, too, and chased squirrels. Out came the canvas and paints once more.

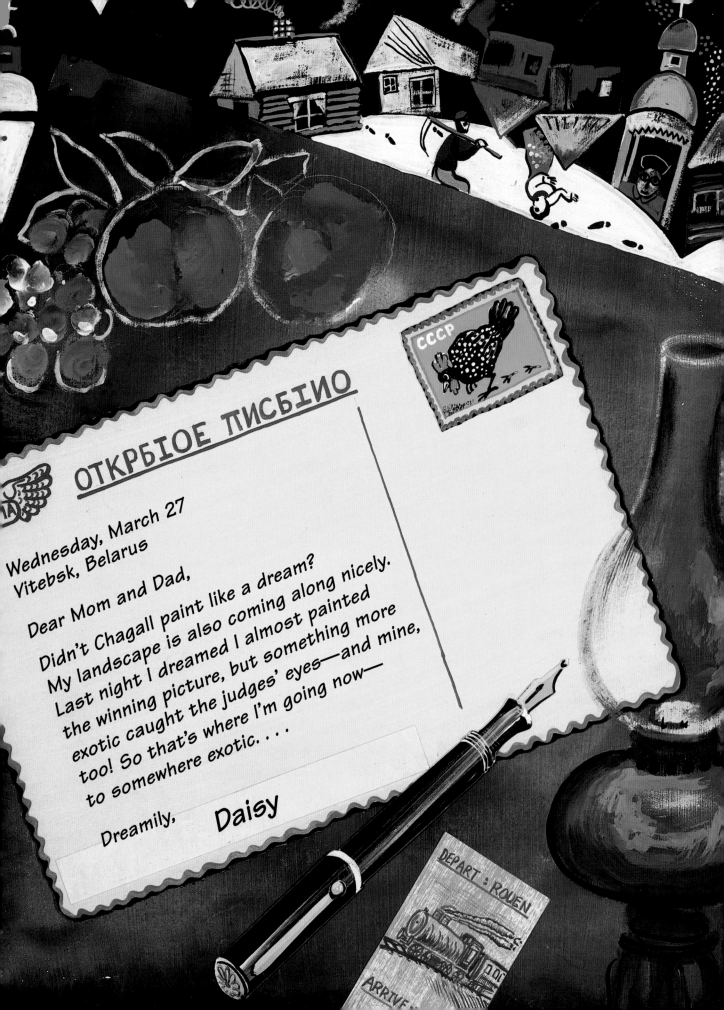

ОТКРБІОЕ ПИСБІИО

Wednesday, March 27
Vitebsk, Belarus

Dear Mom and Dad,

Didn't Chagall paint like a dream?
My landscape is also coming along nicely.
Last night I dreamed I almost painted
the winning picture, but something more
exotic caught the judges' eyes—and mine,
too! So that's where I'm going now—
to somewhere exotic. . . .

Dreamily,     Daisy

*The Poet Reclining* (1915) MARC CHAGALL

Thursday—and Daisy and Duggie were in paradise!
Tahiti was lovely and hot, with big bright parrots,
curious scents, whispering waves, and friendly people.
It took Daisy's breath away. Soon she was busy painting

*Les Artistes des Mers du Sud.*

Thursday, March 28
Tahiti

Dear Mom and Dad,

The tropics are gorgeous, and so are
Gauguin's colors!  He really knew
how to paint the good life. But
paradise is a bit too quiet for me.
I think I like excitement and
action better. . . .

Adventurously,

Daisy

TAHITI

*Where do we come from? What are we? Where are we going?* (1897) Paul Gauguin

On Friday, Daisy and Duggie flew to Wyoming.
The wind whistled from one end of the prairie to the other.
As Daisy tried to paint, everything got blown about.

BLUE POLES
RANCH

WALL STREET JOURNAL
NEW YORK
ART PRICES
PLUMMET
30TH
MARCH

Whoops!  Her easel fell over.
Splat!  Her paint pots went flying.
Now her picture was really looking action packed!

*Blue Poles* (1952) JACKSON POLLOCK

Saturday, March 30
New York City

Dear Mom and Dad,

Wyoming was too windy, so Duggie and I have decided to spend the rest of our trip in New York. I've just seen a great Jackson Pollock picture in a gallery

POLLOCK

57TH ST

TAXI

window. It seems that the world is full of famous painters—so why not me?

If only I could find my favorite things.
See you soon.
Duggie is longing for his bone and basket.

Doggedly,

Daisy

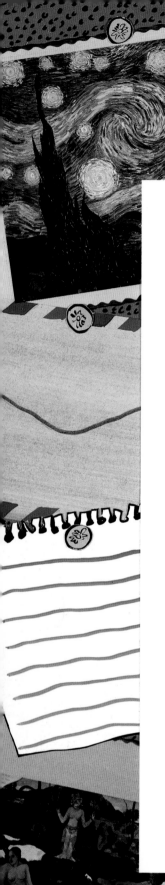

Sunday—at last, Daisy and Duggie
were home! Daisy's mom and dad were
very happy to see them. They had kept all
of Daisy's postcards pinned to the bulletin
board in the kitchen.

Daisy thought her room looked different.
Or was she just seeing it with new eyes?
Little things reminded her of all
the wonderful places she had visited.
It wasn't long before she realized that
her favorite things had been home
all the time.

Later, her mom and dad heard the clatter
of brushes and the squishing of paint.
They peeked through the window and saw
Daisy busy at work on a new painting.
She finished it just before bedtime.

It was Daisy's best painting ever.
Fame at last. . . . Well, almost.  But her mom and dad
were very proud anyway—and so was Duggie!

# About the Artists

### Vincent van Gogh, 1853–1890 *Dutch artist*

In 1888, after painting for a couple of years in Paris, van Gogh moved to the South of France. There he started to produce the thick-brushed, brilliantly colored paintings that have made him a legend. He painted his best-loved works—*Cornfield and Cypress Trees*, *The Starry Night,* and *Sunflowers*—in the two years before he died.

### Claude Monet, 1840–1926 *French artist*

Monet's atmospheric landscapes painted during the 1860s have earned him a reputation as one of the founders of the Impressionist movement. In 1883, Monet created a beautiful garden in Giverny, France, that inspired some of his greatest paintings.

### Marc Chagall, 1887–1985 *Russian artist*

Born in Vitebsk in a country known today as Belarus, Chagall was an experimental painter influenced by the Cubist art movement in Paris. His paintings reflect his Jewish upbringing and influences of Russian folk art. As well as painting pictures, he illustrated books, designed stained glass, and worked as a theatrical designer in Russia, France, and the United States.

### Paul Gauguin, 1848–1903 *French artist*

Brought up in Peru, Gauguin worked with the Impressionists in Paris. In 1891, he went to Tahiti and spent the rest of his life painting the exotic images with the decorative lines and flat bright colors that have made him famous.

### Jackson Pollock, 1912–1956 *American artist*

Born in Wyoming, Pollock worked in New York City, where he became a central figure in the art movement known as Abstract Expressionism. The drip-painting and action-painting methods he used to create his large canvases have strongly influenced modern American painting.